Copyright © 2000,
2002 by Hachette Livre
All rights reserved. Published in the U.S.
by Alfred A. Knopf, a division of Random House, Inc.,
New York, and simultaneously in Canada by Random House
of Canada Limited, Toronto. Distributed by Random House, Inc.,
New York. Originally published in France as Lisa à New York by
Hachette Jeunesse in 2000. KNOPF, BORZOI BOOKS, and the colophon are
registered trademarks of Random House, Inc. www.randomhouse.com/kids
Library of Congress Cataloging-in-Publication Data: Gutman, Anne.
[Lisa à New York. English.] Lisa in New York / Anne Gutman ; illustrated
by Georg Hallensleben. p. cm. Summary: When Lisa gets lost while visiting
her uncle in New York City, she is saved by her own cleverness and a
Statue of Liberty night-light. ISBN 0-375-81119-2 [1. Lost children—Fiction.
2. New York (N.Y.)—Fiction. 3. Statue of Liberty (New York, N.Y.)—Fiction.
4. Uncles—Fiction. 5. Dogs—Fiction.] I. Hallensleben, Georg, ill. II. Title.
PZ7.G9844 Li 2002 E—dc21 00-054956 First Borzoi Books edition:
April 2002 Printed in France 10 9 8 7 6 5 4 3 2 1

ANNE GUTMAN • GEORG HALLENSLEBEN

Lisa in New York

Alfred A. Knopf • New York

I have an uncle who lives in a skyscraper in New York City, and for my birthday he sent me a plane ticket to come and visit him. Uncle Harrison is the best uncle ever!

Every day we went sightseeing. We were always in a hurry because there was so much to see.

The Statue of Liberty. We took a boat to see her. It was very windy!

The Brooklyn Bridge.

And more bridges.

The funny-looking Flatiron Building.

And lots of skyscrapers.

We also went to Central Park. But my favorite place was . . .

. . . Times Square!
We went there to buy my souvenirs.

I found something for my friend Gaspard right away: a Statue of Liberty night-light, even better than the electric gondola that he bought for me in Venice.

We were going to buy a book for my parents.
But on the way to the bookstore, I saw
something wonderful in a store window.

It was a circus made entirely of cake!
I stopped to look at it,
and when I turned around . . .

OH, NO!
My uncle had
disappeared.

I WAS LOST!

But I'm no baby. I knew just what to do. I found a policeman, and he told me to go to the information desk, where they would make an announcement over a loudspeaker to find my uncle.

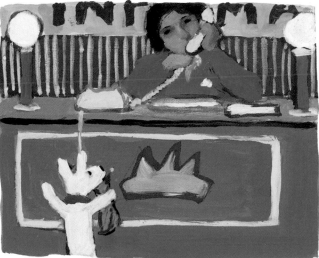

The information lady couldn't see me. I jumped up and down. Then she picked up a phone and a loud-speaker said, "Little Lisa, your uncle is waiting for you on the 64th floor." I was SAVED!

I got on the elevator.
But I had a problem. . . .

. . . I couldn't reach the button for the
64th floor. So I stood on the Statue of
Liberty. Just as I pressed the button,
I heard a loud CRACK.

Oops! Her arm broke.

Then the elevator opened and there was
my uncle! I told him about the circus made
of cake, but I don't think he believed me.
"You have a big imagination," he told me.

But later when he kissed me good night, he promised that we could go back to Times Square tomorrow. I would show him that there really is a circus made of cake!